When It's the Last Day of School

Maribeth Boelts

illustrated by

Hanako Wakiyama

G. P. PUTNAM'S SONS • NEW YORK

Published simultaneously in Canada.
Manufactured in China by South China Printing Co. Ltd.
Designed by Gina DiMassi. Text set in Ad Lib.
The art was done in oil on bristol board.
Library of Congress Cataloging-in-Publication Data
Boelts, Maribeth, 1964-
When it's the last day of school / Maribeth Boelts;
illustrated by Hanako Wakiyama.   p. cm.
Summary: A boy tells how he will change his behavior
on the last day of school.
[1. Schools—Fiction. 2. Behavior—Fiction.]
I. Wakiyama, Hanako, ill. II. Title. PZ7.B635744 Wh 2004
[E]—dc21 00-045908 ISBN 0-399-23498-5
1 3 5 7 9 10 8 6 4 2
First Impression

To my friends at Orchard Hill Elementary School.

—M. B.

To Victor. The husband and boy at heart in my life.

—H. W.

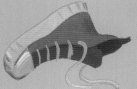

When it's the
last day of school,
this will be me . . .

flying,
jumping,

can't stop smiling,
  running all the way to school . . .
    ME!

When it's the last day of school,
I won't talk to Tony during Silent Reading Time,
or cut in line to sharpen my pencil.
I'll say all the words to the Pledge of Allegiance,
and not skip over the Republic part.

I'll get my drink at the drinking fountain
1,
      2,
            3
                  and not spit the water back out
                  because it's warm.

I'll do all my work, right on time,
and I'll get Mrs. Bremwood's
last gold star sticker for the year.

She'll be amazed that I could do all that work with my
lucky pencil—the one that is just an eraser and a
point. It's the pencil everyone wants, but I tell them
that it takes a lot of standing in line and a lot of
sharpening and a lot of writing to get a
pencil to look like mine.

When it's the last day of school,
I'll only go to the bathroom one time in the morning
and one time in the afternoon, and on the way
back from the bathroom,
I'll just wave to John the Janitor instead of
stopping in his office and asking him about
what he's been cleaning lately and did he
know that the towel machine in the boys'
bathroom was jammed?

At lunch, I'll thank the lady who always smiles at me,
and even the one with the grumpy face,
and I'll tell them that it's a good lunch,
even if it's not.

I'll tear open my straw
and not blow the wrapper off at Tony,
or smash my milk carton,

or show Tiffany Primrose
    how I can burp and talk at the same time.

When it's the last day of school,
I'll watch the film about lizards during science.
I won't think about riding bikes
through the fire-hydrant water with Tony—

or maybe going camping
if we can get a tent,

or finding
    that secret crabbing spot.

I'll sit in my chair and not tip it back,
or put my head in front of the projector,
or laugh with an Outside Voice
because the science guy in the movie
wears weird pants.
I'll think about lizards,
and how they're reptiles,
and what they eat
and how they live in places that are . . .

hot,

like summer,

like what's coming up
when the last day of school
is over.

I'll clean out my desk, and I'll scrub the top of it with paper towels and the spray stuff that smells like my dentist, and I'll give my desk three squirts, not a bunch, just like Mrs. Bremwood says.

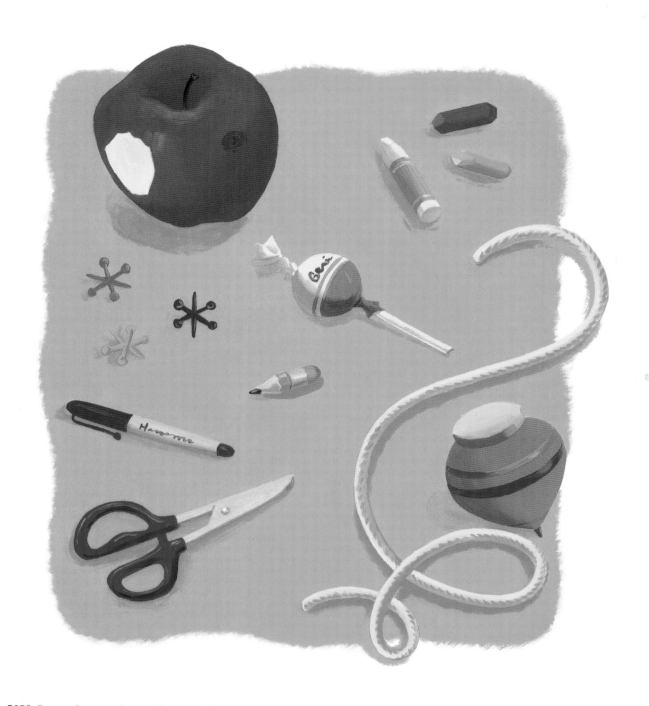

I'll load my backpack with my lucky pencil and my leftover crayons and the markers that work and the scissors that don't and the sucker from a long time ago that I forgot to eat.

When it's the last day of school,
    and the bell rings,
        the last bell—
I'm going to give Mrs. Bremwood
        my strongest hug ever,
            and I'll kind of pick her up a little bit,
                and she'll laugh and say,
"I've so enjoyed having you in class, James.
    Have a wonderful summer."

And then . . .

And then . . .

I'll

EXPLODE!!!!